One of Three

by ANGELA JOHNSON
pictures by DAVID SOMAN

Orchard Books
An Imprint of
SCHOLASTIC INC.

New York Toronto London Auckland Sydney
Mexico City New Delhi Hong Kong Buenos Aires

Text copyright © 1991 by Angela Johnson. Illustrations copyright © 1991 by David Soman. All rights reserved. Published by Orchard Books, an imprint of Scholastic Inc. ORCHARD BOOKS and design are registered trademarks of Watts Publishing Group, Ltd., used under license. SCHOLASTIC and associated logos are trademarks and/or registered trademarks of Scholastic Inc.

ISBN 0-531-07061-1

10 9 8 7 6   7 8 9/0

Printed in the USA   40

First Orchard Books paperback edition 1995. Revised Orchard Books paperback edition 2004.

Book design by Mina Greenstein
The text of this book is set in 16-point Monticello.
The illustrations are watercolor paintings reproduced in full color.

To my beloved grandmother,
the late Mattie Werren Johnson
—A.J.

For Liana
sister, painter, and best friend
—D.S.

Since I can remember I've been one of three.
Eva, Nikki, and me.

One of three sisters that walk to school together.
Down the street together.
One of the three in the sun and the rain.

I'm one of the three that lives in apartment number 2,
has long hair and brown eyes, and can sometimes
play hopscotch by the trash cans
if I ask for a long time.

On Saturdays I'm one of the three that sits
outside the bakery and looks and smells and smells….

I'm one of the three that squeezes into the taxi
on snowy days with Mama, Aunt Sara, and Grandma,
and it's warm there.

I'm one of the three that looks just like our mama,
smiles just like our daddy,
and holds hands with my sisters in the store,
looking like triplets—almost.

I'm one of the three that likes the subway,
the people on it,
and the way our feet hang over the seats.

I'm one of three who lives over the flower shop.
Mr. Lowen still gets all of our names wrong,
but he gives us each a daisy every time.

We walk down the street like stairsteps,
and I'm in front.

Sometimes Eva and Nikki say I'm not invited to go with them. Not to the park, the store, or sometimes even for a walk.

I'm left behind.
Not one of three, just one.

Then Mama calls me Sister and says I'm too little
to go there or do that,
so maybe I just want to help her paint or read to her.

Daddy says that I have to be the baby sometimes,
and keep Mama and him company,
just sometimes.

I miss Eva and Nikki and me....
But when it's just Mama, Daddy, and me,
it's a different kind of three,
and that's fine too....